Baboo

For my husband David, who spurred me on
to write Mary's story — A M
To my parents, Steve, Phil and Kim for their
love and encouragement — B W

With thanks to Margaret M. Cohoe, who shared her remarkable "Mary"
research with me; and to Louise Reynolds whose book *Agnes, The Biography
of Lady Macdonald* inspired me; and to the staff of Bellevue House who
showed me Mary's typewriter. — A M

My thanks to John Grenville, Bellevue House; Veronica Goodenough and
the British High Commission; Sandy Allen, Rideau Hall; and the National
Archives of Canada. — B W

Text copyright © 1998 by Ainslie Manson
Illustrations copyright © 1998 by Bill Wand

Groundwood Books / Douglas & McIntyre
585 Bloor Street West, Toronto, Ontario M6G 1K5

Distributed in the U.S.A. by Publishers Group West
4065 Hollis Street, Emeryville CA 94608

We acknowledge the support of the Canada Council for the Arts and the
Ontario Arts Council for our publishing program.

Canadian Cataloguing in Publication Data

Manson, Ainslie
Baboo : the story of Sir John A. Macdonald's daughter

ISBN 0-88899-329-3

1. Macdonald, Mary Margaret Theodora, 1869-1933—Juvenile literature. 2.
Macdonald, John A. (John Alexander), Sir, 1815-1891—Family—Juvenile
literature. 3. Handicapped women—Canada—Biography—Juvenile literature. 4. Hydrocephalus—Patients—Canada—Biography—Juvenile literature
I. Wand, Bill, 1967- . II. Title.

FC521.M32M36 1998   j971.054092   C97-932730-X
F1033.M36 1998

Back cover photograph courtesy the National Archives of Canada
Printed and bound in China by Everbest Printing Co. Ltd.

BABOO

The Story of
Sir John A. Macdonald's
Daughter

———

by Ainslie Manson

with pictures by Bill Wand

A GROUNDWOOD BOOK

Douglas & McIntyre § *Toronto Vancouver Buffalo*

Sir John A. Macdonald was not like other fathers. His daughter Mary knew that. Only one father in the whole wide world was the first prime minister of Canada.

And Mary was not like other daughters. She knew that, too. She would never be able to walk, she had difficulty speaking, and she even found it hard to use her hands.

Mary Margaret Theodora Macdonald was born with a brain injury. Her father and mother hoped and prayed that some day she would be able to run and play like other children, but when they realized this would never happen, they learned to rejoice at each small improvement.

Mary was a gentle, thoughtful person, and though she spent her whole life in a wheelchair, she rarely complained. Her mother, Agnes Macdonald, once wrote to a friend, "She has all her father's charm of kindly grace and everyone loves her."

Mary thought her papa was wonderful. At the end of each day she would have her wheelchair placed at just the right angle by the window so she could watch for the carriage bringing him home from the Houses of Parliament.

Usually Sir John would burst in the door and without even stopping to remove his hat, he would lift his daughter onto his lap for a cuddle and a story.

But being prime minister of Canada was not an easy job, and sometimes he came home late, weary and in need of unwinding. At these times Mary would wait patiently as he sat by the fireside, soaking up the warmth and trying to forget the worries of the world.

Generally it wasn't long before he would be chatting and joking again. He would even crawl around on the drawing-room floor, being silly and making Mary laugh.

Mary was proud when her papa patted her on the head and said, "You have my curls, Mary," or tweaked her on the nose and said jokingly, "Baboo, I think you've inherited my nose!" (Only her papa called her Baboo!)

Each morning Mary was carried to her parents' room while they were still in bed. This was her favourite time of day. She would snuggle down under the comforter, warm and happy. Papa always had a story for her before he began his busy schedule.

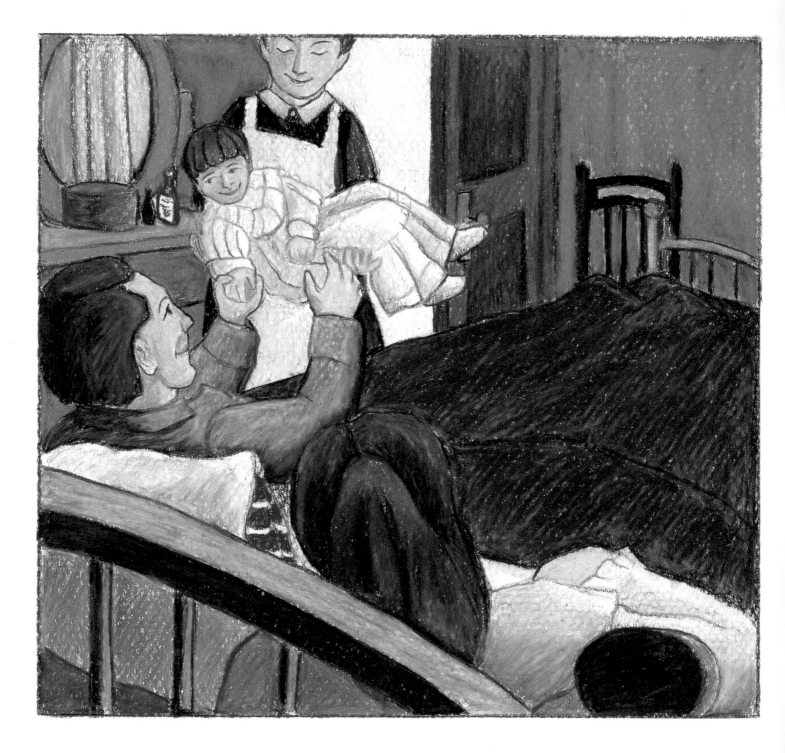

The Macdonalds lived in Ottawa in a big grey stone house called Earnscliffe. Important people often came to dinner, and Mary would listen to their conversations.

She especially liked to hear about Queen Victoria, who was not only queen of England but also queen of the Dominion of Canada.

Two years before Mary was born, Queen Victoria had knighted her papa. On Canada's birthday, July 1, 1867, he had become SIR John A. Macdonald.

Political issues were regularly discussed and debated at Earnscliffe. Mary decided that the politics of the government of Canada were far from easy to understand!

Her mother once said, "Here...in this house...the atmosphere is so awfully political that sometimes I think the very flies hold parliaments on the kitchen table."

Lady Macdonald frequently visited the House of Commons when Parliament was in session. She and Sir John had learned sign language so that they could send secret messages back and forth from the gallery to the floor!

On one occasion Lady Macdonald took Mary with her. Mary was proud when her tall, distinguished father rose to his feet to speak. She had no difficulty understanding his speech. It was short and full of the kind of funny stories Mary loved to hear him tell. As a rule, his speeches were short, but she had been told that one time her papa had spoken in the House for five hours without stopping! Lord Dufferin, who was governor general of Canada at that time, said Macdonald had "electrified the House with this tremendous oration."

Sir John frequently had to be away from his Baboo. He often visited the other Canadian provinces, and a few times he even travelled by ship all the way to England to meet with the queen. At these times, Mary missed him dreadfully. But whenever father and daughter were apart, they would write letters to one another.

One summer it was Mary who was away from home. She and her grandmother were in Rivière-du-Loup, Quebec, and Sir John wrote this letter to her from Earnscliffe:

My dearest Mary,
You must know that your kind Mama and I are very anxious to see you and Granny again. We have just put a new carpet in your room and got everything ready for you.

The garden looks lovely just now. It is full of beautiful flowers and I hope you will see them before they are withered.

There are some fine melons in the garden. You must pick them for dinner and feed the chickens with the rind. You remember that Mama cut my hair and made me look like a cropped donkey. It has grown quite long again. When you come home you must not pull it too hard.

I intend to have some new stories for you when you come in the morning into Papa's bed and cuddle him up.

Give my love to dear good Grand Mamma and give her a kiss for me...and so goodbye my pet and come home soon to your loving papa.
John A.

Mary loved her papa's letters. They made him seem not quite so far away. She would always reply immediately. But since her hands didn't work very well, she had to dictate her letters:

My dear Father,
I sit down to write to you in my Uncle's room. I hope you are quite well. Your wife Agnes sends her love. She did not tell me to say so but I am sure she would if she knew it.

I have a little dog that my Uncle gave me. Dear Father, when are you coming back? I hope you will be back soon for Agnes misses you very much and says often to me "how I wish my husband was back".

The house seems so dull and lonely without you and I miss my evening stories very much.

...I hope you are having a fine time down there. Agnes will be down to you on Monday. She is going somewhere on Monday, but I don't know where to. Perhaps it is to you, dear Father. I hope you are very well...
Believe me,
Your affectionate Baboo and daughter.
Mary Macdonald

Oh! What a scrimmage I've made. I forgot to say anything about my old hen. Sarah is well and chirpy as ever. That's all.

When writing letters, Mary always had the words in her head, but sometimes she found it hard to make herself understood when she was dictating a letter. She wished there was some way she could put the words on paper by herself.

Sometimes Mary would sit in her wheelchair on the wide deck of Earnscliffe, gazing out at the Ottawa River. She would remind herself that she must not become discouraged. She would pick up the feltwork lying idle on her lap and work a little harder at it. Gradually she found it easier to use her right hand, though it was still impossible to write.

Mary's friends meant a great deal to her, and she was invited to all kinds of social functions. She was often a guest at Rideau Hall, the home of the governor general of Canada. The five Dufferin children frequently put on plays. Mary was unable to take part in the performances, but she was always an enthusiastic member of the audience.

Once she was invited to assist at a charity bazaar held at Rideau Hall. She and teenaged Nellie Dufferin sold flowers together in one of the main stalls.

Mary attended parties and dances, too. A frequent guest at the same parties was the distinguished inventor and scientist Sandford Fleming. He was Canada's foremost railway surveyor and construction engineer and one of Mary's favourite grown-up friends. At one party, he bowed to her gallantly and asked her to dance! Mary laughed with delight as he held her upright in his strong arms. Together they joined the other children in a ring dance.

Music was extra special to Mary. She would sit for hours, as quiet as a mouse, listening to a piano recital or a concert. When the renowned Canadian-born singer, Madame Emma Albani, came to town, she not only stayed at Earnscliffe, but she sang especially for Mary on her birthday!

Mary loved birthdays—everyone's birthday, not just her own. She would attend friends' birthday parties and they would attend hers.

Mary's parents had a birthday ball for her when she was in her teens. When Sir John saw how much she was enjoying herself, he encouraged the orchestra to keep playing and the guests to stay longer. When the colourful dancers were again circling the floor, he whispered in his daughter's ear, "You see, Baboo, they want a little more of your society and a little more dancing by the way."

Once when her papa could not be home for his birthday, Mary celebrated anyway. She had a party in his honour and more than eighty guests came to toast her famous father.

"Here's to Sir John, our first prime minister!"

"Here's to Sir John, a dreamer of dreams that come true!"

"Here's to one nation from sea to shining sea, and linked by the iron rails..."

"Here's to my papa. I wish you were here."

But the very best birthday Mary ever had was the birthday
when Papa placed a big, heavy, oddly shaped package on the table
before her. She could not begin to guess what was inside...

Papa and Mama helped her unwrap the gift, but even when she saw it, she didn't know what it was!

"A new invention," Papa explained. "A typewriting machine, or typewriter. Now you can write your letters all on your own, Baboo!"

Mary was thrilled, and from that time on she wrote all her own letters. She could use only her left index finger and two middle fingers of her right hand, and so each letter took a great deal of time, but Mary had a great deal of patience!

She wrote to her friends, she wrote to her aunt and to her uncle. And most important of all, she wrote to her papa when he was away, using her own words and putting her letters together just the way she wanted them.

AFTERWORD

Mary Margaret Theodora Macdonald was twenty-two years old when Sir John died. She and her mother were lost and lonely in Ottawa without him. They tried living in various parts of Canada but eventually moved to England. Mary adored London. She liked the bustle and excitement of Hyde Park, museums, the aquarium and the Crystal Palace, but best of all she loved the theatre. She would attend performances whenever possible. They spent several winters in Alassio, Italy, but Mary was happiest in London.

Mary was fifty-one years old when her mother died. She lived the rest of her life with her maid-companion, Sarah Coward. "My Coward," Mary called Sarah, and they were great friends. When Sarah married, Mary went on living with her and her husband.

Mary never visited Canada again, but using her beloved typewriter, she kept in touch with many of her Canadian friends and family members. Mary lived to sixty-four. This was an exceptional age in those days for a person with Mary's physical disabilities. Certainly all the love, care and encouragement that she received throughout her life helped to make this possible. She is buried in Hove, England.